TAS, GEM AND BEC AROUND THE PINE TREE

93

Tas and Gem wake up.

Time to play.

Tas and Gem run around the pine tree.

Bec can fly around the pine tree.

The pine tree is wide and green.

The pine tree is in the garden.

Tas, Gem and Bec sit around the pine tree.

Gem, Tas and Bec are happy together.

Gem, Tas and Bec are so cute.

Tas and Bec like to listen to Gem.

Gem can say garden words.

Gem can say, pipe and pile.

pipe

pile

Gem can say, gate.

Tas likes the gate.

gate

Bec listens.

Bec can say pipe, pile, gate.

pipe

pile

gate

In the garden there is a pile of rocks.

In the garden there is a water pipe.

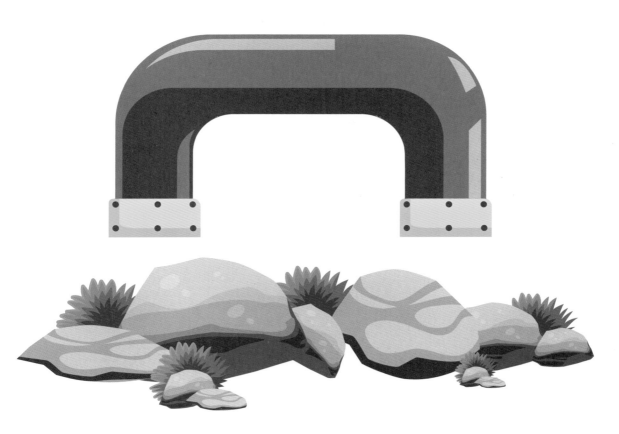

In the garden there is a gate.

Tas likes to sit by the gate.